F IS FOR FUFU

AN ALPHABET BOOK BASED ON THE GHANAIAN GOLDILOCKS

by Dr. Tamara Pizzoli
Illustrated by Phil Howell

For
Noah, Milo, Mamma & my beloved Nappy
and the village that helped publish The Ghanaian Goldilocks...
and the fantastic Phil Howell.

ISBN - 978-0-9960016-2-5

Cover Design and Illustration by Phil Howell www.philhowelldesign.com

F IS FOR FUFU

AN ALPHABET BOOK BASED ON THE GHANAIAN GOLDILOCKS

by Dr. Tamara Pizzoli
Illustrated by Phil Howell

A IS FOR

AKWAABA

GHANA

AKWAABA

You are welcome, the Ghanaians say,

You are welcome in our home, this land

Today and always.

B IS FOR BABIES

Tied snugly on their mama's backs,

They laugh and look and even nap

While mama does this and that.

IS FOR
CAPE COAST

Come on and stay awhile,

We'll go to market, walk on the beach

And chat and fish and smile.

D IS FOR
DREADLOCKS

Worn by some but not all,

These beautiful twists of coily hair

Can be kept short or very long.

E IS FOR EL MINA CASTLE

A place with a dark past,

It serves today as a reminder

Of what happened when the focus was on caste.

F IS FOR FUFU

A truly delectable dish,

But put that fork and spoon away-

You may use your fingers, if you wish.

G IS **FOR**

FOR GOLD COAST

The name Ghana used to hold,

For Ghana is rich in many resources,

Including cocoa, diamonds and gold.

H IS FOR HANDSTANDS

There's time and space to do a few,

You think you can stay up longer than me?

Eh ya, show me what you can do.

I IS **FOR** INSTRUMENTS

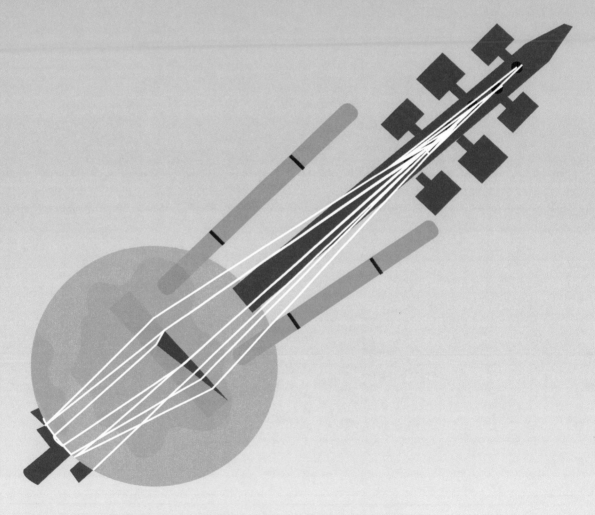

Some handmade and others we buy,

Don't throw that calabash away,

We'll make a Kora and strum awhile.

J IS FOR JOLLOF RICE

It's not so hard to make.

You'll need spices, tomatoes, rice, and veggies

Then salt and pepper to taste.

K IS FOR KENTE CLOTH

A vibrant fabric woven by hand on looms,

We'll pick the color, style and pattern

To match the occasion and our moods.

L IS FOR
LOVE AND LAUGHTER

Oh, in Ghana there's tons!

Eti sen? How are you?

is a question to ask everyone.

M IS FOR MOVING BOXES

You will need them if you go

Back and forth from Kumasi to Accra

Like the residents of the Osei home.

N IS FOR
NASSIMA

Akuffo's wife & Kwaku's mother;

There are just three people in the Osei home.

Kwaku doesn't have little sisters or brothers.

O IS **FOR**
OSEI FAMILY

Just how will they react

When they return and suddenly find

That their home is not in tact?

P IS FOR POMBO

A game that Ghanaian children play.

We'll need seven stones, now toss one in the air,

Pick another one up and catch it-Hooray!

Q IS FOR QUICK DECISIONS

We all eventually have to make.

When the Oseis find Kofi in their home

will he run or stay? There's a lot at stake.

R IS FOR RECIPES

Are you hungry? Shall we whip up something new?

Can I interest you in fried fish or kenkey?

How about some red red stew?

S IS FOR

STOOL

A noble seat carved carefully out of wood,

There are many types from which to pick-

Choose wisely, like a king or queen would.

T IS FOR
TOMATOES

A staple of the Ghanaian diet,

There are so many dishes we can make

Like this spicy tomato paste, just try it!

U IS FOR UPSIDE DOWN

Mama Nassima got a strong clue

That someone had been in the Osei home

From the position of her shoe.

V IS FOR
VEGETABLES

So many good kinds to eat,

Carrots, bell peppers, yams for sure-

What's your favorite veggie treat?

W IS FOR

WARDROBE CLOSET

No beds in this Goldilocks tale

The designs on each closet door

Have countless stories to tell.

X IS FOR XYLOPHONE

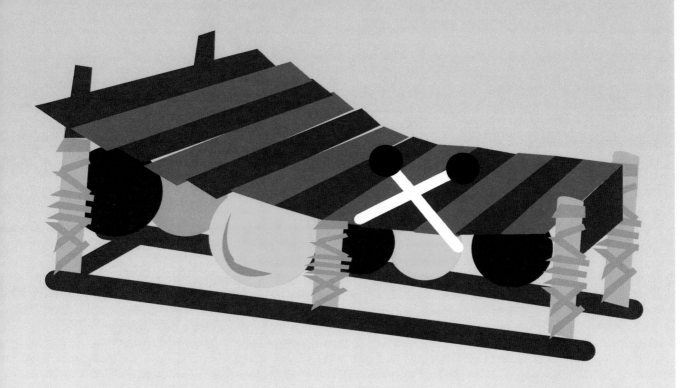

Made from natural things...

3 calabashes, some wood, and a bit of bamboo-

What a lovely sound-ding ding!

Y IS FOR
YAW

Ye fro wo sen? What's your name?

This is Yaw, he runs a coconut stand,

His wife is called Elaine.

Z IS FOR

ZITHER

An instrument that's part of Kwaku's collection,

Next time you're in Ghana stop by his house to play-

Now THAT would be perfection.

Made in the USA
Monee, IL
04 October 2021